I've Got Music!

by Cathy Molitoris
Illustrated by Sarah McConnell

Scholastic Inc.
New York   Toronto   London   Auckland   Sydney
Mexico City   New Delhi   Hong Kong   Buenos Aires

D0473031

To Marty, Claire, and Charlotte,
who put the music in my life.—C.M.

For Rich, who has music, too!—S.M.

ISBN 0-439-88620-1

Text copyright © 2006 by Scholastic Inc.
Illustrations copyright © 2006 by Sarah McConnell.

12 11 10 9 8 7 6 5 4 3 2 1   6 7 8 9 10 11/0

BOOK DESIGN BY JANET KUSMIERSKI

Printed in the U.S.A.
First printing, October 2006

Cora was a little girl who loved music—

not the kind of music you or I love,
although she did enjoy a good piano recital.
Instead, Cora loved the music
she heard all around her every day.

She loved to **TAP TAP TAP**
her feet to the **PAT PAT PAT**
of rain on her bedroom window.

She loved to hum along to the low
BUZZZZ of the refrigerator.

DRUM DRUM DRUM went her fingers on her knees while she sat in the car.

CLICK CLICK CLICK went her tongue on the roof of her mouth as she listened to the thumping beat of the clothes dryer.

Cora couldn't imagine a life without music
or drumming or clicking,
but plenty of people around her could.
When she **SPLISH-SPLASHED**
her feet to the beat in the bathtub,
she sometimes **SPLISH-SPLASHED**
water all over the bathroom.

"Let's keep the water inside the tub," her mother would sigh.

When the tapping of her feet on the kitchen floor distracted her father from reading his paper, he would say, "Cora, please keep quiet."

At soccer practice, she would puff her cheeks in and out with the rhythm of sneakered feet as they swooshed on the grass.

"Cora," her coach would command when the ball sailed past her. "Concentrate on the game, please."

Still, nothing could stop Cora from **TAPPING, CLAPPING,** and **SNAPPING.** She tried to keep the music to herself, but it was hard.

Then one day, Cora's mommy brought a baby sister home from the hospital. Cora couldn't believe how tiny she was! All she did was sleep, eat, cry, sleep, eat, cry.

And she cried a lot. She cried in the morning.
She cried in the evening. She cried all night.

Cora tried to concentrate on
her music, but it was hard to do.
The crying drowned out
all the usual noises in her house.

Cora complained to her mother.
"Babies cry," her mother said.
"You just have to get used to it."

She complained to her father.
"Try to ignore it," he said.

Cora sat on her bed and pouted.
She tried to hum a tune, but it wasn't
easy. She couldn't hear anything but
"**WAH WAH WAH!**" over and over
and over again.

Finally, she got up and went into her *sister's* room.

"For a little baby, you make a big noise," she scolded. "Why can't you just be quiet?"

Her sister stopped crying, looked at Cora, and started crying again.

Cora turned to leave the
room, but then suddenly
she stopped.
She listened carefully.
Could it be? she wondered.
Was it possible?

Could her sister's crying actually sound like music?

Cora had to admit the crying had a rhythm to it.

WAH! WAH! WAH!

Before she knew it, Cora began to **TAP! TAP! TAP!** her feet on the floor.

She started to **SNAP! SNAP! SNAP!** her fingers.

And she **HUMMED** a soft tune.
Then she **HUMMED** a little louder.

Soon she was
TAPPING,
SNAPPING,
and **HUMMING**
with gusto.

Then something amazing happened.
Cora's sister stopped crying.
She watched Cora with fascination.
Slowly, she began to smile.
Then she began to **GIGGLE**
and **WIGGLE**.
She kicked her feet
and waved her arms.
She **SQUIRMED** with delight
and squealed with joy.

And Cora smiled a giant smile because she knew right then that she had finally found someone who appreciated her music as much as she did.

With all the **COOING** and **GIGGLING**,
Cora didn't just have a new baby sister...

SHE HAD A BAND.